D0577372

IS IT PURIM YET?

CHRIS BARASH

Pictures by
ALESSANDRA
PSACHAROPULO

ALBERT WHITMAN & COMPANY
CHICAGO, ILLINOIS

When spring's waking up
from its deep winter sleep

And from warm cuddly burrows
small heads start to peep...

Purim is on its way.

When we fill hamantaschen with Gran's wooden spoon

And she asks with a big smile, "strawberry or prune?"

Purim is on its way.

When we pack special baskets with goodies to eat

As holiday gifts for our friends down the street...

Purim is on its way.

When from Aunt Clara's bag a
noisemaker appears

And that grogger's so loud
our pup covers her ears...

Purim is on its way.

When Mom takes from the closet a Queen Esther gown
And then helps us create a great Mordecai crown...

Purim is on its way.

When we think of the people who need help and care
And then count the tzedakah box coins that we'll share...

Purim is on its way.

When the synagogue fills with a big, happy crowd

that shouts when they hear Haman's name said out loud...

When we read the Megillah
scroll's wonderful news

that Queen Esther's great bravery protected the Jews...

Purim is here!

Celebrate throughout the year with other books in this series!

Is It Passover Yet?   **Is It Hanukkah Yet?**   **Is It Sukkot Yet?**

To my sweet sister, Clara—CB

To my parents—AP

Library of Congress Cataloging-in-Publication data
is on file with the publisher.

Text copyright © 2016 by Chris Barash
Pictures copyright © 2016 by Alessandra Psacharopulo
Published in 2016 by Albert Whitman & Company
ISBN 978-0-8075-3391-8
All rights reserved. No part of this book may be reproduced or transmitted in any
form or by any means, electronic or mechanical, including photocopying,
recording, or by any information storage and retrieval system,
without permission in writing from the publisher.

Printed in China
10 9 8 7 6 5 4 3 2 1 LP 20 19 18 17 16

Design by Morgan Avery

For more information about Albert Whitman & Company,
visit our web site at www.albertwhitman.com.